Sando

サンド

Sando

A story about a young man,
an egg sandwich,
and the quiet place where joy lives.

Michael Keith Williams

Sando

This is a work of fiction. The characters, organizations, and events portrayed in this novel are either products of the author's imagination or are used fictitiously.

Illustrations by Michael Keith Williams
Cover design and typesetting by CoverKitchen

ISBN 979-8-9952640-0-2 (paperback)

This book is for anyone

who has ever walked past their peace

without knowing it was there.

You are precious.

No matter how small you feel in the world.

Special thanks to Yumi, whose handmade matcha and generous spirit made this book possible.

And whose hand guided the Japanese
that lives within these pages.

And to Bria — thank you for leading me there.

There was a young man
who was always moving.

Not because he had somewhere to be,
but because he was afraid
of what might happen if he stopped.

He had been taught that life was about doing.
More. Faster. Louder.

And he believed it,
the way you believe something
you have never thought to question

One morning, he walked down a street
he had walked down a hundred times
and noticed a door he had never seen.

It was small.
The sign above it said:

Yumi's Coffee
ユミズコーヒー

A sunflower bloomed from a coffee cup on the logo.

The door was open just enough
to let two things drift out into the morning:

the scent of freshly ground coffee,
and the soft, unhurried sound of jazz.

He went in.

The jazz did not greet him the
way most music does—
demanding attention, filling every corner.
It simply made room for him.

A piano, brushed drums, a bass
walking slowly beneath it all
like a heartbeat that had learned patience.

The kind of music that doesn't ask
if you like jazz.
It just invites you
to like where you are.

Inside, there were only eight seats.

おいしいコーヒーの店

Calligraphy on the wall.
Plants climbing shelves.
A clipboard menu written by hand.

And on a mini side table near the window,
so small you might miss it—

a tiny origami crane.

Its wings were no wider than a thumbnail.
It sat perfectly still,
as if it had landed there on purpose
and decided to stay.

Behind the counter stood a young woman
whose movements were so calm
they seemed to belong to the music—
measured, intentional,
every gesture arriving right on the beat.

"Irasshaimase," she said.
Welcome.

Her name was Yumi.

She made everything by hand.
The coffee. The baked goods.
The small beautiful things in the glass case
that looked less like food
and more like someone's way of saying
I made this with care. For you.

He noticed another origami figure
on the ledge near the register.

A tiny fox, sitting upright,
no bigger than a thimble.

He almost asked about it.
But something about its smallness
made him feel it was not meant to be explained.

It was meant to be noticed.

He ordered a Kuromitsu Matcha Latte
with oat milk.

He did not know what kuromitsu was.
But the menu described it as
a dark sugar syrup from Okinawa,
made from unrefined black sugar—
sweetness that has not forgotten where it came from.

And then he watched Yumi make it.
She did not rush.

First, a fine mesh sieve
held over a ceramic pouring bowl.

She tapped the matcha powder through it
the way you might sift flour for something sacred—
slowly, deliberately,
breaking every tiny clump
so the powder fell like green dust
into the bowl below.

Then, hot water.
Not boiling. Just below.
Poured in a thin stream
that turned the powder
into something alive.

Then the whisk.

A bamboo chasen,
its fine tines worn soft with use.
Yumi moved it in quick, small strokes—
not circular but back and forth,
like someone writing a letter
they wanted to get exactly right.
The matcha began to froth.

A thin layer of foam rose to the surface,
pale green, delicate,
like the first light of morning
forming on still water.

She added a few drops of agave
into the mixture—
just enough to soften the bitterness
without erasing it.

A little sweeter. That was how he liked it.

Then she reached for a plastic cup
and filled it with ice.

It was a warm day.
The kind of day that makes you want
something cold to hold.

She poured in the oat milk first—
white and calm over the ice.

Then she took the kuromitsu
and swirled it along the inner edges
of the cup—
a slow, deliberate ribbon
of dark Okinawan sweetness
tracing the glass like calligraphy.

And last, the matcha.
Poured from the ceramic bowl
in a steady green stream
that sank through the milk
and swirled into something
you could not look away from—
green and white and dark
layered like a landscape
seen from very far above.

She set the cup before him.

The whole thing had taken two minutes.
It had felt like a ceremony.

He had never seen anyone
treat a drink this way.

As if it mattered.
As if he mattered.

As if the act of making something well
for someone you just met
was not a transaction
but a form of welcome.

When it was time to pay,
he reached for his card.
But there was no machine held out to him.
No impatient hand extended.

Instead, on the counter,
a small wooden tray.

Bamboo. Simple. Polished by years of use.

Yumi waited.
He placed his card on the tray.
She lifted it with both hands,
completed the transaction,
and placed it back on the tray
for him to take.

Their hands never touched.
And yet the exchange
felt more personal
than any handshake he had ever known.

There was a space between them
that honored both.

This is how care moves in Japan.
Not by closing the distance,
but by making it sacred.

And then he saw, in the glass case,
a row of small sandwiches.
White bread, crustless, cut into triangles.
Golden filling visible through the cut face.

Tamago sando.
Egg sandwich.

The young man took a bite
and sat very still.

The bread was so soft it yielded like a sigh.
The egg was cool and golden
and tasted like someone's patience.

The chill of it was part of the kindness—
kept cold with care,
the way you protect something delicate
so it arrives to the person whole.

He took a sip of the matcha.
The dark kuromitsu rose through the green
like smoke through jade.

A saxophone joined the piano—
not loud, just present,
the way a good friend enters a room
without needing to announce themselves.

And for the first time in a very long time,
he did nothing.

He did not check his phone.
He did not plan tomorrow.
He did not rehearse what he
should have said yesterday.

サンド

He just sat there,
in the company of jazz
and a tiny paper crane
and the taste of something honest.

And something inside him
that had been clenched for years
quietly opened.

There are many kinds of sando in Japan.
The katsu sando—golden pork cutlet,
crisp and bold, a celebration in bread.
The fruit sando—strawberries and cream
pressed between shokupan like stained glass.
The wagyu sando—rich,
extravagant, unapologetic.

But the tamago sando is none of those things.

It is quiet.
It is simple.
It does not try to impress you.

SPRING

春

He came back the next week.
And the week after that.

Each time, he ordered the same thing.
Kuromitsu Matcha Latte. Oat milk.
Tamago sando.
The seat by the window.

And each time, the jazz was different.
Some mornings it was piano and bass only—
a conversation between two old friends
who had run out of things to prove.

Other mornings a trumpet floated above it all,
delicate and searching,
like a bird that was not lost
but simply exploring.

The music never repeated.
But it always felt like the same invitation.

He began to notice the origami.
They were everywhere—
not cluttering the space,
but inhabiting it.

A miniature turtle on the shelf by the sugar.

A paper rabbit near the napkins.

A folded butterfly
balanced on the rim of a small ceramic vase.

Each one was impossibly tiny.
Each one was impossibly careful.

As if someone had taken a scrap of paper
and said to it:
You may be small.
But I will make you into something beautiful.

There were newer things on the menu.
Seasonal specials. Treats he had not tried.
Yumi's baked goods changed with the weeks—
each one a small work of art.

But he kept choosing the egg sandwich.

"You always order the same thing,"
Yumi said one morning.
"I know," he said.
"Why?"

He thought about it.

The jazz shifted beneath them—
a key change so gentle
it felt like the room breathing in.

"Because it doesn't ask me to be
anyone other than who I am."

Yumi smiled.
It was the kind of smile that said
I understand.

Spring is the season of beginning again.
Not beginning from nothing—
beginning from where you already are.
With what you already have.
With whatever small, quiet thing
has been waiting for you to sit down
and receive it.

SUMMER

夏

In summer, the world outside moved fast.
Everyone was busy.
Everyone had plans.
Everyone was on the way to somewhere else.

Inside Yumi's, the matcha came iced.
The kuromitsu settled at the bottom of the glass
like a secret, waiting to be stirred.

The jazz moved slower in the heat—
a lazy bass, a cymbal shimmering
like sunlight on still water.

The tamago sando was cold from the case,
and that was its gift.

A new origami figure had appeared
on the side table near his seat.
A tiny elephant.
Ears unfolded like open hands.

He stared at it for a long time.
Something about its smallness
made him feel enormous.

Not in size.
In worth.

"What is ikigai?" the young man asked.
He had seen the word on a small card
pinned to the wall near the window.

Yumi set down the cup she was drying.
"It is the reason you wake up," she said.
"Not because you have to.
Because something in you is already awake."

"How do you find it?"
"You don't find it," she said.
"You notice it.
It has been there the whole time."

She glanced at the tiny elephant on the side table.
"Like those?" he asked.
"Like those," she said.
"Small does not mean unimportant.
Small is how precious things begin."

He looked at the half-eaten sando in his hand.
He looked at the matcha, the
swirl of dark and green.
He looked at the light through the window.

The piano played a phrase so tender
it sounded like someone forgiving themselves.

He thought:
Maybe ikigai isn't something you build.
Maybe it's something you allow.

That summer, he watched Yumi work.
She arranged her baked goods in the glass case
with the care of someone placing flowers—
each item positioned with intention,
each morning begun with the same quiet ritual.

"Did you come here to build something big?" he asked.
"No," she said.
"I came here to take care of something small."

She folded a napkin into a triangle
and placed it beneath a fresh madeleine.
"Every precious thing starts that way."

And he understood.
Joy is not loud.
Joy is the quiet place
that opens inside you
when you stop performing your life
and start living it.

Like jazz.
You don't have to understand it
to feel it in your body.
You just have to let it play.

秋

AUTUMN

秋

Autumn was his favorite.
Not because anything extraordinary happened,
but because the world seemed to exhale.

The mornings arrived cooler.
The light through the window
fell differently on the counter—
longer, softer, more golden.
As if the sun itself
had decided to slow down.

The jazz in autumn had more depth.
The way a cello joins a quartet—
not to take over,
but to say something
the higher instruments could not.

Even if you didn't like jazz,
you would like this room.
The music made you grateful
just to be sitting somewhere.

Yumi made chestnut madeleines in autumn.
Sweet potato scones with amber glaze.
Treats that appeared and disappeared
with the season, like small goodbyes.

But the tamago sando stayed.
And the Kuromitsu Matcha Latte stayed.

And he stayed.
A new origami figure sat on the windowsill.
A tiny owl.
Its head was tilted,
as if listening to the music.
Beside it, an origami leaf,
folded from paper the color of rust.

He picked up the owl
and held it in his palm.
It weighed almost nothing.
And yet it felt like the most important thing
he had held in months.

Precious.
That was the word.
Not impressive. Not grand.
Precious.

The origami.
The sandwich.
The matcha.
The jazz.
This room.
This moment.

You are a work of art
no matter how small
you feel in the world.

There is a Japanese word: mono no aware.
It means the bittersweet awareness
that beautiful things do not last.
It is not sadness.
It is the understanding that we can feel
the passing of something lovely,
and that our ability to feel it
is what makes us alive.

One October afternoon, the shop was nearly empty.
The jazz was just piano now—
slow, deliberate, like someone
choosing their words very carefully.
"Yumi," he said. "Why do I keep coming here?"
She did not answer right away.

She finished slicing a row of tamago sando
into perfect triangles.

"Because," she said,
"you found the space that was yours."

"What do you mean?"
"Everyone has one," she said.
"A place where the noise stops.
Where you can hear yourself again.
Most people walk past it.
You walked in."

They sat in the quiet for a while.
The jazz held them both—
a slow piano, a brush on cymbal,
the room breathing.

"Yumi," he said. "What does your name mean?"
She smiled.
"It depends on how you write it," she said.
"In Japanese, a name can hold
many meanings at once."

*beautiful reason, beautiful friend,
graceful beauty, kind ocean,
kind sea, bow.*

"Yumi can mean beautiful reason.
Or beautiful friend.
Or graceful beauty."

She paused.
"Or it can mean bow—
the archery bow.
In kyūdō, the art is not about the target.
It is about the form. The breath.
The presence."

"The act of drawing the bow
is the meaning."

He looked at her—
this young woman
who sieved matcha like a ceremony,
who placed each baked good like a flower,
who returned a debit card with both hands
as if it were something borrowed and sacred.

Beautiful reason.
Beautiful friend.
Graceful beauty.
The bow drawn with presence.
All of it was true.
All of it at once.

And he thought about names.
How a name is not just a word.
It is a signature.
The way God places
a unique thumbprint
on each individual life—
like the brushstroke
of a finely crafted paintbrush
on a canvas no one else will ever carry.

Your name is not an accident.
It is part of His signature on you.
Written before you arrived.
Waiting for you to grow into its meaning.

He looked at the tiny origami owl
on the windowsill.
It had no name.
And yet it was precious.

Imagine, then,
how precious you are—
you who were given one.

He took a bite of the tamago sando
and closed his eyes.

The piano held a single note
and let it ring.

It tasted like a gentle hug.
The kind that says:
There is peace on this earth.
You just have to sit still long enough
to let it find you.

WINTER

冬

In winter, he came more often.
Not because he needed shelter.
Because winter is the season of stillness,
and stillness was where
he did his deepest listening.

The jazz in winter was the most beautiful.
It played the way snow falls—
without effort, without destination,
each note arriving exactly when it should
and disappearing without regret.

A brushed snare. A muted trumpet.
A bass so low
you felt it more in your chest
than in your ears.

It asked nothing of him.
It gave everything.

That is the complexity of jazz.
It sounds simple
until you realize
how much courage it takes
to leave that much space between the notes.

Yumi added something to the matcha in winter.
A whisper of yuzu.
You would not know it was there
unless you were paying
the kind of attention
that most people save for emergencies
but that joy requires every day.

On the small side table by the door,
a new origami figure had appeared.
A person.
Not a crane or a fox or an owl.
A tiny folded human being,
standing with arms slightly open,
as if waiting to embrace something
or someone.

He stood in front of it for a long time.
And he thought:
That is what it feels like to be here.
Arms open. Receiving.

The tamago sando in winter
was the same as it was in every season.
And that was exactly the point.

In a world that insists on novelty,
in a world that says faster, newer, more—
the tamago sando simply was.

Bread. Egg. Care.

It did not need a winter edition.
It did not need a limited release.
It just needed someone
to sit down and receive it.

One afternoon, a man at the next table
looked up from his book and said,
"This is the best coffee shop in the city
and nobody knows about it."

The young man smiled.
That is exactly the point.

The places that change your life
are never the ones everyone knows about.
They exist at the frequency
of your own particular need,
tuned to a wavelength
that only your soul can receive.

God does not broadcast His gifts
on loudspeakers.
He tucks them into corners of the world
where only the person they were meant for
will find them.

A small coffee shop
with a sunflower on the logo.
An egg sandwich
made with love.
A dark sweet drink
that tastes like somewhere
you have not been yet,
but that feels like home.

Jazz that doesn’t explain itself
but makes everything make sense.

A tiny paper figure on a side table
that says, without words:
You are precious.

These are not accidents.
These are arrangements.

再び春

SPRING AGAIN

Spring returned,
as spring does,
without asking permission.

He walked through the door.

The brass bell chimed.
The jazz welcomed him
the way it always did—
not with fanfare,
but with a chair pulled out
and a place already set.

Yumi looked up and smiled
and did not ask what he wanted.
She already knew.

He watched her make it.
The same ritual.
The fine mesh sieve
over the ceramic bowl.
The green powder falling like dust
through morning light.
The hot water, poured in a thin stream.
The bamboo whisk,
its quick strokes pulling foam
from the surface
like coaxing a whisper from silence.

The drops of agave,
because she remembered.

The ice in the cup.
The oat milk, white and calm.
The kuromitsu swirled along the edges—
that slow dark ribbon.

And the matcha poured through it all,
green sinking into white,
layering itself into something
he had seen a hundred times
and would never tire of watching.

Nothing had changed.
The sieve. The water. The whisk.
The agave. The ice.
The milk. The dark ribbon. The green stream.
And yet everything had changed.

Because the first time he watched it,
he was a stranger
learning to be still.

And now he was someone
who understood
that the ritual was never about the drink.
It was about being worth
the care it took to make it.

He placed his card
on the small wooden tray.
Yumi lifted it with both hands.
Returned it the same way.

The same sacred space
between giver and receiver.
The same quiet honor.

A year ago, it had confused him.
Now it felt like the truest thing
he knew about love.

Leave space.
Handle gently.
Return with both hands.

She placed the tamago sando on a plate
and set it beside the matcha.

He sat by the window.
The tiny crane was still there.
Wings no wider than a thumbnail.
Still as the day he first noticed it.

And he realized
he had become like the crane.
Small. Still.
Exactly where he was supposed to be.
And precious.

Outside, the world moved
at its usual frantic pace.
Inside, time moved differently.

At the speed of matcha
dissolving into kuromitsu.
At the speed of bread
yielding to the press of teeth.
At the speed of a jazz note
hanging in the air
just long enough
to mean something.
At the speed of a person
remembering who they are
when no one is asking them to perform.

He took the first bite
and closed his eyes.

There it was.
The gentle hug.

Every human being on earth
has been given this gift.

A space.
A moment.
A taste.
A slant of light at a particular hour
that falls on a particular surface
and makes you feel,
for just an instant,
that everything is going to be all right.

Not because the world is perfect.
The world is far from perfect.

But because God,
in His infinite kindness,
has wrapped a personal package
for each of us.

It contains exactly the peace we need.
In exactly the form we can receive it.

Sometimes it looks like a tiny paper crane.
Sometimes it sounds like a piano
playing to an almost-empty room.
Sometimes it tastes like egg and bread
and dark sweet matcha
and the quiet attention of someone
who made something beautiful
just because it was morning.

Yours is out there too.

Perhaps you have already found it
and do not yet know its name.
Perhaps you walk past it every day.
Perhaps it is waiting for you
on a shelf in a place
you have not yet entered,
made by hands you have not yet met,
wrapped in a simplicity
the world has trained you to overlook.

It is small.
It is quiet.
It is yours.
And it is precious.

Go find it.
Sit with it.
Let it be enough.

Yoi ichi nichi wo.
Have a good day.

Sando

Written and illustrated by
Michael Keith Williams

www.ingramcontent.com/pod-product-compliance
Lightning Source LLC
LaVergne TN
LVHW052308100826
845147LV00006B/702

9798995264002